YETIS ARE THE WORST!

ISBN 978-1-339-03446-1

Copyright © 2022 by Alex Willan. Book design by Chloë Foglia © 2022 by Simon & Schuster, Inc. All rights reserved. Published by Scholastic Inc., 557 Broadway, New York, NY 10012, by arrangement with Simon & Schuster Books for Young Readers, an imprint of Simon & Schuster Children's Publishing Division. SCHOLASTIC and associated logos are trademarks and/or registered trademarks of Scholastic Inc.

12 11 10 9 8 7 6 5 4 3 2 1   23 24 25 26 27 28

Printed in the U.S.A.   40

First Scholastic printing, September 2023

The text for this book was set in Rockwell.
The illustrations for this book were rendered digitally.

For my Dad

TOP SECRET!

Nothing to see here

YETIS ARE THE WORST!

BY ALEX WILLAN

GILBERT'S SECRET HIDEOUT

Pssst! Over here.

KEEP OUT!

Shhhhhh

SCHOLASTIC INC.

YETIS

ARE SO COOL

and MYSTERIOUS

etcetera etcetera

Like the Tooth Fairy,

What does she do with all of those <u>teeth</u>?

gnomes,

How do they keep their hats so pointy?

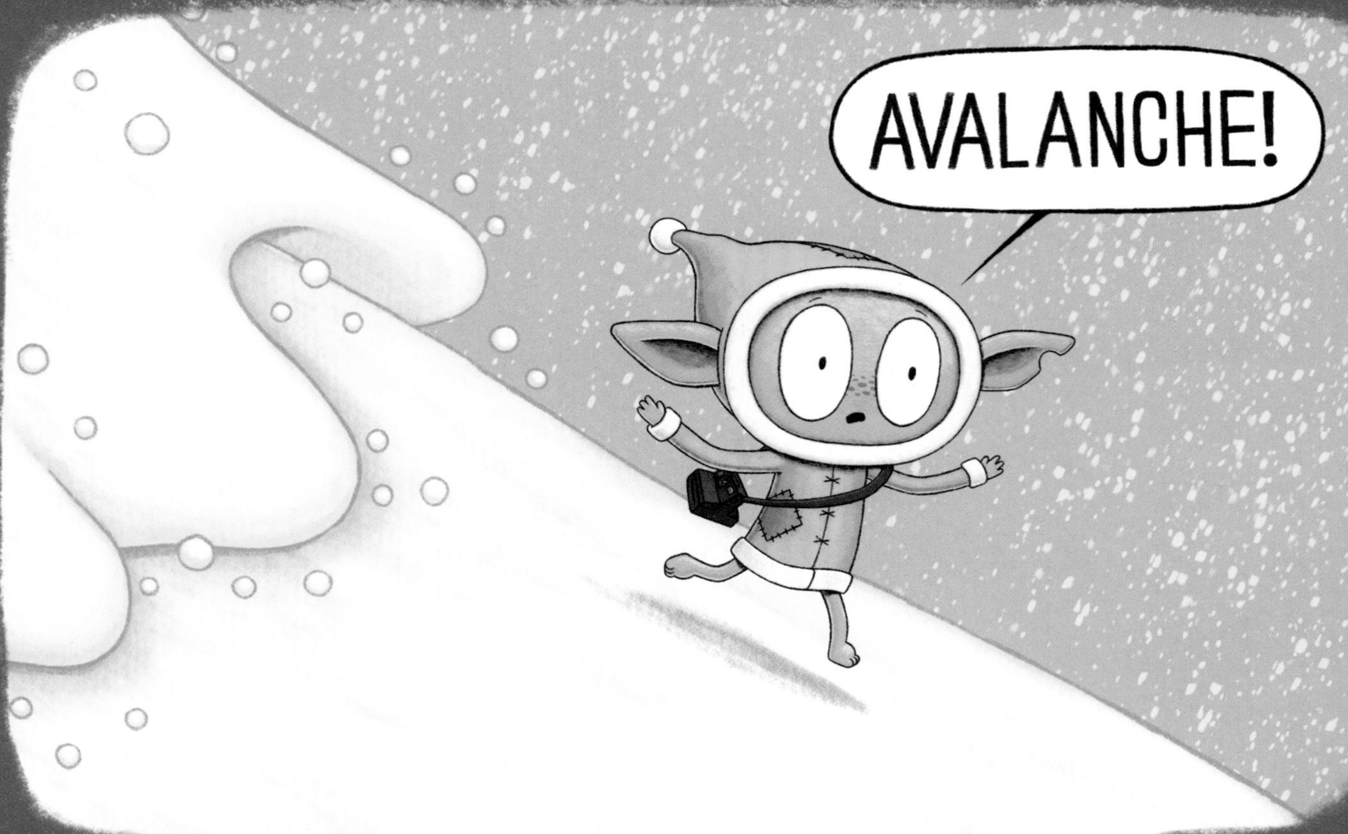
AVALANCHE!

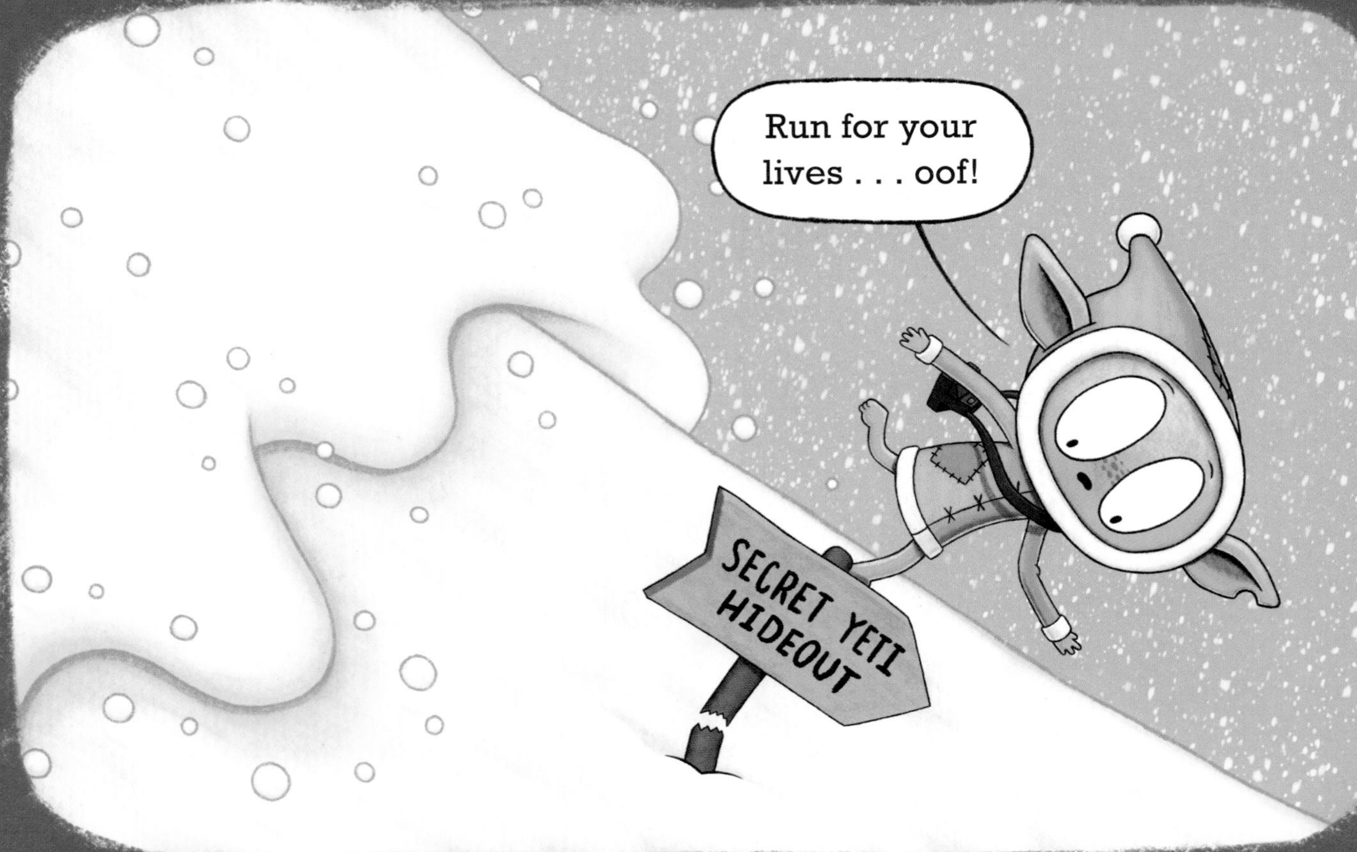
Run for your lives . . . oof!
SECRET YETI HIDEOUT

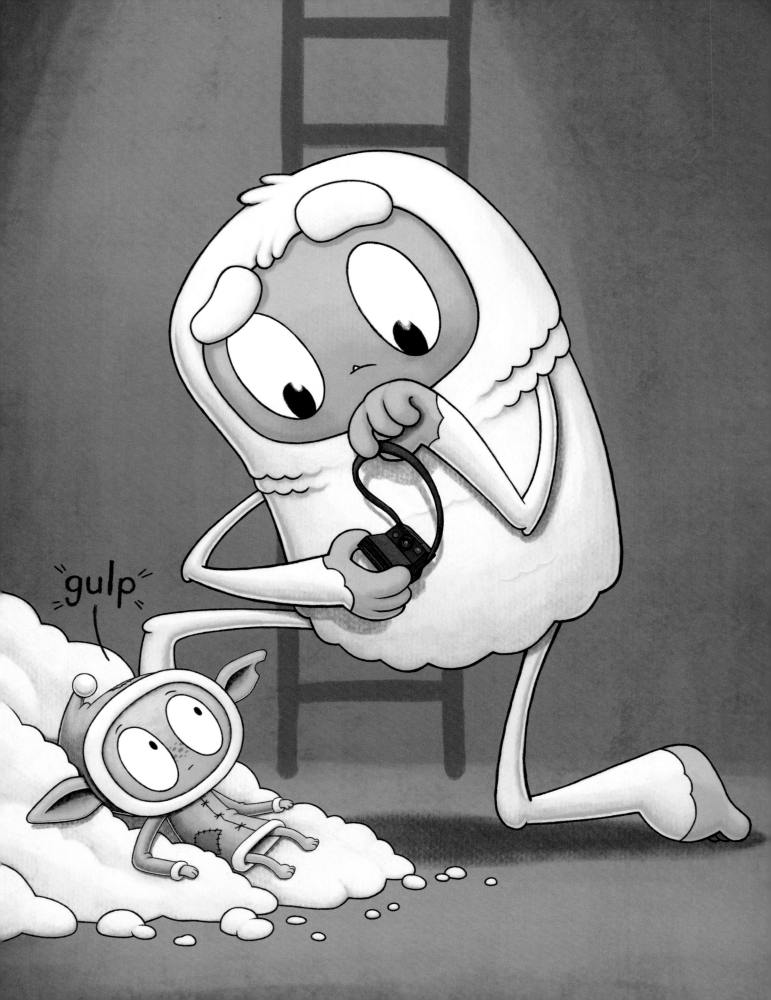

If it was **ALEX WILLAN**, and *not* Gilbert the Goblin, who was in charge of writing the stories, he'd make a book called *Anchovies Are the Worst!* Alex is the author-illustrator of *Unicorns Are the Worst!*, *Dragons Are the Worst!*, and the Jasper & Ollie series, as well as the illustrator of *Got Your Nose*, written by Alan Katz. Alex lives in Chicago with his dog, Harley, who is the absolute best.

Gilbert the Goblin is the first to admit that he was, ahem, mistaken— unicorns actually throw the *best* tea parties, and dragons make *delicious* ice cream soup. This time, though, he can confirm that YETIS ARE ABSOLUTELY THE WORST!

Sure, they may *seem* cool and mysterious, but Gilbert is certain that once you meet one, you'll find they're not all they're cracked up to be! And that's what Gilbert plans to do: meet a yeti. That is, if he can find one. . . .

But how hard can that be?

You're in this one too?

SCHOLASTIC

www.scholastic.com

ISBN 978-1-338-89106-5

$7.9

50

9 781338 891065

13-BUS-571

A Tale of Shakespeare's Dog

CRAB & WILL

WRITTEN & ILLUSTRATED
BY
GREGORY MAGNUSON